Sabrina
the Sweet Dreams
Fairy

Special thanks to Narinder Dhami

ISBN 978-0-545-31661-3

12 11 10 9 8 7 6 5 4 3 2 1   11 12 13 14 15/0

Printed in the U.S.A.   40

This edition first printing, September 2011

Sabrina
the Sweet Dreams
Fairy

by Daisy Meadows

SCHOLASTIC INC.

New York Toronto London Auckland
Sydney Mexico City New Delhi Hong Kong

The Night Fairies' special magic powers
Bring harmony to the nighttime hours.
But now their magic belongs to me,
And I'll cause chaos, you shall see!

In sunset, moonlight, and starlight, too,
There'll be no more sweet dreams for you.
From evening dusk to morning light,
I am the master of the night!

Contents

Nightmares!

"Oh, isn't it sad that this is our last night at Camp Stargaze, Kirsty?" Rachel sighed as she snuggled down inside her sleeping bag. She glanced up at the black sky overhead, where tiny silver stars were glittering like diamonds. "Still, having an outdoor sleepover is a wonderful way to end our vacation together!"

Kirsty nodded as she unzipped her own sleeping bag and climbed in. "It's been fun, hasn't it, Rachel?" she agreed. "I'm so glad we came!"

The girls and their parents were spending a week of summer vacation at Camp Stargaze, which got its name because it was in a wonderful place to view the night sky. It was a warm, clear evening, and all the children had brought their sleeping bags onto the grassy area by the tents. They'd had milk and cookies, and Peter, the camp counselor, had read them a bedtime story.

"OK, time to turn off your flashlights now," Peter called. "Good night, everyone."

"I want to come back to Camp Stargaze again next year," said Lucas. He and Matt, two of Rachel and Kirsty's new friends, were lying on the lawn in their sleeping bags near the girls. "It's the best vacation I've ever had!"

"I learned a lot about the stars from Professor Hetty," Matt declared, turning off his flashlight. "And I'm going to keep reading about them when I get home, too. Good night, Rachel and Kirsty!"

"Good night," the girls called.

All the flashlights were turned off now, and the camp was in darkness except for the pale light of the moon. Gradually, everything fell silent, other than the occasional gentle hooting of an owl in the Whispering Woods nearby.

"Nobody else knows that this has been an extra-magical vacation for us, Kirsty," Rachel whispered, smiling at her friend in the moonlight.

"Yes, we've had some amazing fairy adventures!" Kirsty whispered back.

After the girls had arrived at Camp Stargaze earlier that week, their fairy friends had asked them to help once more. Rachel and Kirsty had been

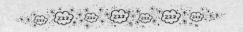

horrified to learn that Jack Frost and his goblins had stolen seven satin bags of magic dust from the Night Fairies while the fairies were at an outdoor party.

The Night Fairies used their magic to make sure that the hours between sunset and sunrise were peaceful and harmonious, just as they should be. But with the magic bags in the hands of Jack Frost and his goblins, all kinds of strange things had been happening, including a green sunset and the stars moving around in the sky!

"I know we've found six of the bags," Rachel said, "But there's still one fairy left to help—Sabrina the Sweet Dreams Fairy."

Rachel, Kirsty, and the Night Fairies

had been determined to find the bags of magic dust after Jack Frost's icy magic had sent his goblins spinning into the human world to hide the bags there. So far, the girls and the fairies had outwitted the goblins over and over again. They had retrieved almost all of the bags!

"Let's hope we can find Sabrina's bag tomorrow before we go home," Kirsty said with a yawn. "Good night, Rachel."

"Good night, Kirsty," Rachel replied.

A few minutes later, Kirsty heard her friend breathing deeply and knew she was asleep. Kirsty cuddled down in her sleeping bag, feeling comfortably warm and drowsy. She gazed up at the sky, but suddenly she noticed that the light of the moon had vanished. For a moment,

Kirsty thought the moon had slipped behind a cloud, but then it reappeared for a second or two before disappearing again. It was almost like someone was flipping a switch and turning the moon off and on, Kirsty thought, feeling confused.

Then she saw that the stars were moving. They were zooming around the night sky,

mixing up all of the constellations. It made Kirsty dizzy just watching them.

Suddenly Kirsty heard a cold, icy chuckle. It sounded so close that it sent a shiver down her spine.

"Ha, ha, ha! Those silly girls and their pesky fairy friends are no match for me this time!" Jack Frost gloated. "I have ALL the Night Fairies' magic bags, and now I am the master of the nighttime hours!"

"Hooray for Jack Frost!" the goblins cheered.

"No!" Kirsty gasped. "This can't be happening. . . ."

Suddenly Kirsty shook herself awake. She had broken out in a cold sweat and was tangled up in her sleeping bag.

"Oh, I was dreaming!" Kirsty sighed with relief. "I didn't even realize I'd fallen asleep. What a terrible nightmare!" She glanced at Rachel and

was surprised to see her friend sitting up,
yawning and pushing her hair out of
her eyes.

"Are you OK, Kirsty?" Rachel asked.
"I just had an awful dream about Jack
Frost and the goblins. . . ."

In the Starry Glade

"Oh, so did I!" Kirsty exclaimed, and she quickly told Rachel about her dream.

"My nightmare was that Jack Frost kidnapped all the Night Fairies and locked them in his Ice Castle," Rachel said with a sigh. "It seemed so real. . . ."

"I think it might be because Sabrina the Sweet Dreams Fairy's bag of magic dust is missing," Kirsty pointed out. "Should we go to the snack tent and make some hot chocolate? It might help us sleep."

"Great idea," Rachel agreed.

The girls slipped silently out of their sleeping bags, trying not to wake the other kids who seemed to be sound asleep. Then they tiptoed across the camp to the snack tent. Rachel grabbed two mugs, and Kirsty spooned some chocolate powder into them.

As the girls went over to the hot water

thermos, Lucas's mom stepped into the
tent. She was carrying Lucas's younger
sister, Lizzy, who was sobbing loudly.

"Oh, poor Lizzy!" Kirsty said. "What's
wrong?"

"I'm not sure," Lucas's
mom replied, giving
Lizzy a comforting
hug. "I think she
must have had a
nightmare. She woke
up crying and talking about
'greenies,' whatever they are."

Kirsty and Rachel glanced at each
other as Lucas's mom went to get Lizzy
some warm milk. "Greenies," Rachel
repeated. "Do you think Lizzy was
dreaming about goblins, Kirsty?"

"It sounds like it," Kirsty replied,

frowning as she added hot water to their
mugs. "There are a lot of bad dreams
around tonight, aren't there, Rachel?"

"Like you said before, this must be
because Sabrina's bag is missing!"
Rachel said.

The girls took their mugs of hot
chocolate and sat on a bench outside the
snack tent under the stars.

"Look, Rachel," Kirsty said after
taking her first sip of hot chocolate.
"Here comes your dad."

Rachel glanced across the camp and saw her father. He'd just come out of the tent the Walkers and the Tates were sharing, and now he was wandering toward the girls. But as he got closer, Rachel and Kirsty could see that something was wrong. Rachel's dad didn't seem to have noticed the girls, even though he was staring straight at them. He looked kind of dazed and upset.

"What's the matter with him?" Rachel asked, feeling worried. "Kirsty, do you think he's sleepwalking?"

Before Kirsty could reply, Mr. Walker stopped abruptly. He blinked a few times and shook his head as if he were trying to clear it. Then he noticed Rachel and Kirsty staring at him.

"Oh, hello, girls," Mr. Walker said, rubbing his eyes. He glanced down at his pajamas, looking confused. "What am I doing out here?" he asked.

"I think you were sleepwalking, Dad," Rachel told him. "Are you all right?"

"I'm fine," Rachel's dad reassured her, "but I was having a very strange nightmare. I dreamed that I was surrounded by little green creatures with long noses and big feet! Then I heard cackles of icy laughter, and I felt very cold." He shivered.

Rachel and Kirsty exchanged glances.

"Well, I'd better get back to bed," Mr. Walker said with a yawn. "And you should, too. We've got a long day ahead of us tomorrow. Good night, girls. I just hope I don't have any more nightmares!"

"Good night," Rachel and Kirsty replied as Mr. Walker went back to the tent. Then they turned to each other, eyes wide.

"Jack Frost and the goblins are getting into people's dreams!" Kirsty gasped.

"What are we going to do, Rachel?"

"I don't know," Rachel sighed. "I guess we should go back to our sleeping bags and wait for the magic to come to us. But I don't want to fall asleep again in case I have another goblin nightmare!"

The girls finished their hot chocolate, washed out the mugs, and then tiptoed back across the camp. But before they reached their sleeping bags, Kirsty stopped dead, clutching Rachel's arm. "Look, Rachel!" she whispered. "See that light in the Whispering Woods?" Rachel stared through the darkness, and then she saw it. A tiny, dazzling light was floating

through the woods, weaving its way between the trees.

"Do you think it could be Sabrina?" Rachel asked. Excitement flooded through her.

"Let's go and see!" said Kirsty.

The girls quietly left the camp and slipped into the Whispering Woods, keeping their eyes fixed on the bright light flitting around in the distance. It wandered here and there, not seeming to be headed anywhere in particular.

"I wonder where it's going?" said Rachel.

Suddenly, the light dipped down to the ground, out of sight.

"I think it landed in the Starry Glade," Rachel guessed. "Come on, Kirsty!"

The Starry Glade was a little clearing

in the Whispering Woods, covered with white, sweet-scented, star-shaped flowers. Rachel and Kirsty dashed into the clearing and saw that the light had settled on a springy cushion of green moss. "Kirsty, it *is* Sabrina!" Rachel exclaimed in a low voice as they tiptoed closer.

Sabrina the Sweet Dreams Fairy was fast asleep on a bed of moss among the starry flowers. She didn't even open her eyes as the girls bent over her.

"I wonder why Sabrina didn't come to find us?" Kirsty whispered.

Rachel frowned. "You know how my

dad was sleepwalking?" she reminded
Kirsty. "Well, I think Sabrina might
have been sleep-flying! She was
wandering all over the Whispering
Woods, and she didn't seem to know
where she was going."

Then Sabrina stirred a little. "Help!"
she murmured in her sleep. "Help me!"

Rachel and Kirsty glanced anxiously
at each other.

"Even Sabrina's having a bad dream,"
Kirsty said. "We'd better wake her up,
Rachel!"

Ice Castle Mission

"Sabrina," Rachel called gently. "Wake up. You're having a nightmare!"

For a moment, Sabrina didn't move. Then she slowly opened her eyes and stared up at Rachel and Kirsty.

"Oh, girls, I'm so glad to see you!" Sabrina said shakily. She sat up, pushing her silky brown hair out of her face.

"I was dreaming that Jack Frost had captured me and locked me in a cage made of ice!"

"Lots of people are having nightmares

about Jack Frost and the goblins, including me and Rachel," Kirsty told her, sighing.

"Jack Frost is using my bag of magic dust to give us all bad dreams!" Sabrina exclaimed, looking very upset. She fluttered off her cushion of moss, smoothing down her purple ruffled skirt. "India the Moonstone Fairy taught me how to use my dream magic. But now it's all gone wrong! I have to get my bag back so I can make sure everyone has good dreams again."

"Is the bag somewhere around here in

the Whispering Woods?" Rachel asked eagerly.

Sabrina shook her head. "No, Jack Frost was so angry when the goblins lost the other six bags that he took the seventh bag back to his Ice Castle," she explained. "And now he's guarding it himself!"

Rachel and Kirsty glanced at each other in dismay.

"Girls, will you come to Fairyland with me and help me get my bag of magic dream dust back?" Sabrina asked. "You know that time will stand still here in the human world while you're away."

"Of course we'll come," said Kirsty. "Rachel and I don't

want to have any more awful goblin nightmares, either!"

Smiling, Sabrina lifted her wand and a puff of sparkling fairy dust whirled around the girls. Once again, Rachel and Kirsty felt the familiar rush of excitement as they shrank down and became fairies with their own glittering wings on their backs. Then, with another flick of Sabrina's wand, they zoomed off to Fairyland in a swirl of rainbow-colored magic.

It was nighttime in Fairyland when
Sabrina and the girls arrived! Sabrina
swooped through an open window in
the Fairyland Palace and into the throne
room. Rachel and Kirsty were right
behind her. To the girls' surprise, King
Oberon and Queen Titania were awake
and pacing up and down the room.
King Oberon wore a magnificent purple
robe, while the queen was dressed in
a white silk nightgown. The other six
Night Fairies were there, too, all looking
anxious.

"Oh, girls, thank goodness you found Sabrina and woke her up!" Queen Titania exclaimed, rushing over to hug them. "We have to get the bag of magic dream dust back. The king and I can't sleep because we're having the most terrible nightmares about Jack Frost and the goblins!"

"Yes, I dreamed that Jack Frost stole my golden crown and wouldn't give it back," King Oberon said with a sigh.

"I had a horrible dream that Jack Frost became king of Fairyland, and the goblins were running around the palace gardens pulling the heads off the roses and paddling in the Seeing Pool!" the

queen told the girls.

"And look out there." The king pointed
out the window at the toadstool houses
surrounding the castle. Some of them
were lit up by a bright firefly light. As
the girls and the fairies watched, more
and more lights began to come on in the
other houses.

"It looks like all of Fairyland has
woken up from bad dreams!" Sabrina
said sadly. "But Rachel and Kirsty have
agreed to come to Jack Frost's Ice Castle

with me to try and get the bag back."

The king, the queen, and the six Night Fairies looked relieved.

"You've both come to our rescue once again, girls," said Queen Titania gratefully. "Thank you so much." "And the other Night Fairies will do their best to make sure nothing else goes wrong here or in the human world before morning," the king added. "Take care, all of you."

Quickly Sabrina, Rachel, and Kirsty fluttered out of the palace window again. Then they headed across Fairyland to Jack Frost's Ice Castle.

The girls had been to the Ice Castle before, but as they fluttered through the darkness toward it, it was still a cold, scary sight. The castle was built of sheets of ice with six tall frosty towers. It glittered and gleamed like marble in the pale moonlight.

As Sabrina led the girls toward the castle walls, they heard gruff goblin voices. Immediately, Sabrina put a finger to her lips. There was a group of goblins standing on the castle battlements talking to one another. Sabrina, Rachel, and Kirsty floated down a little lower so they could listen.

"I'm tired," one of the goblins complained with an enormous yawn. "I want to go to bed."

"Jack Frost said we have to guard the castle against fairies—and those human girls!" another goblin reminded him.

Rachel and Kirsty glanced at each other. They could see goblin guards on all the entrances into the castle. How were they going to get past the goblins and slip inside?

Suddenly, one of the goblin guards happened to glance upward. He spotted Sabrina and the girls before they could duck out of sight, and he gave a shriek of anger.

"Look!" he yelled. "Pesky fairies!"

Night Monsters

All the goblins howled with rage and rushed toward Sabrina and the girls. The three friends quickly flew up and out of reach. Then Sabrina began to sing in a sweet voice:

When the sun has set at last,
When the sky is darkening fast,
When the moon is pale and light,

When the silvery stars are bright,
That's the time to rest your head
And climb into your cozy bed,
Sleep and dream the night away,
Tomorrow is another day!

As Sabrina sang her lullaby, the goblins stood staring up at her. Then they all began to yawn and rub their eyes. Rachel and Kirsty watched with a smile as the goblins began to sink down onto the ground, curling themselves up into balls as they fell fast asleep.

"Your magic lullaby worked, Sabrina!" Rachel whispered as she and Kirsty flew down to join the fairy.

"Not quite," Sabrina said with a frown. She pointed at one of the goblins who had stuck his fingers in his ears so  that he couldn't hear the lullaby. "I'm not listening! I'm not listening!" he chanted, running toward them. "Quick, girls, into the castle!" Sabrina cried.

The three friends swooped through the nearest entrance and inside the Ice Castle.

"Stop!" the goblin shouted, chasing them.

"Where's Jack Frost?" Rachel asked as they flew down an icy hallway.

Sabrina frowned. "I don't know," she

replied. "Let's try the Throne Room."

Sabrina, Rachel, and Kirsty zoomed to
the Throne Room and peeked inside, but
Jack Frost's icy throne was empty. The
goblin was still right behind them, so
they kept flying.

"STOP!" the goblin yelled again.
Leaping forward, he
tried to grab Sabrina.
Luckily, he missed.
"Maybe Jack
Frost's in bed?"
Kirsty suggested.
"After all, it is
nighttime."

"But the Ice Castle is huge!"
Rachel groaned as they turned another
corner. The goblin followed them,

panting loudly. "His bedroom could be anywhere!"

Suddenly, the goblin skidded to a halt on the icy floor. "I'm going to tell Jack Frost that you're here," he announced. "Then you'll be in big trouble!" He turned and scurried up a winding staircase of ice in one of the tall towers.

"What luck!" Sabrina whispered with a wide grin. "The goblin's going to lead us straight to Jack Frost! Follow him, girls. But keep out of sight."

Rachel, Kirsty, and Sabrina flew up the staircase after the goblin, keeping far

behind him so he couldn't see them.

They peeked around the corner at the top of the stairs and saw the goblin come to a stop. He was at the very top of the tower, in front of a closed door.

"Look at the sign on the door," Sabrina whispered. "I think we found Jack Frost!"

Rachel and Kirsty stared at the sign. It said: JACK FROST'S PRIVATE CHAMBER.

KNOCK BEFORE ENTERING! The goblin knocked on the door. There was a pause, and then Jack Frost stammered, "C-c-come in!"

Kirsty was surprised. "Why does Jack Frost sound so scared?" she murmured to Sabrina and Rachel.

The goblin went into the room, and
Sabrina and the girls flew in behind him.
Through the darkness, they could see
Jack Frost sitting up in bed, a frightened
look on his face. He wore white pajamas
with a blue snowflake pattern, and he
was holding a blue teddy bear with icy,
spiky fur. A night light was next to him
on the bedside table.

"I came to tell you that there are fairies
in the castle—" the goblin began. But

Jack Frost had already spotted Sabrina, Rachel, and Kirsty, and the frightened look vanished from his face. With a

roar of anger, he grabbed his pillow and clutched it tightly. "I'm in charge of the nighttime now!" Jack Frost declared firmly. "And you'll never get the last bag of magic dust back!"

"Why aren't you asleep?" Kirsty asked, still wondering why Jack Frost had looked so frightened.

The goblin whirled around and glared at her. "Jack Frost never sleeps at night, didn't you know that?" he snapped. "He's scared of the—"

Jack Frost gave a yelp of rage and threw his teddy bear at the goblin. "Get out!" he shouted.

The goblin scurried out of the bedroom as fast as he could.

"Why are you so scared?" Sabrina asked Jack Frost.

Jack Frost frowned. "Nighttime's very dangerous!" he muttered. "There are Night Monsters everywhere—and they'll get you if you go to sleep!"

"Where are the Night Monsters?" Kirsty wanted to know.

"Everywhere!" Jack Frost replied with

a shudder. "Under the bed. In the closet.
In the dresser. Even in my slippers!"
And he pointed down at a pair of icy,
curly toed slippers beside the bed. "They

keep me awake with bad dreams, and
if I have to suffer"— Jack Frost scowled
—"then I want to ruin nighttime for
everyone else, too!"

Sabrina glanced at Rachel and Kirsty. Her eyes were wide. The girls looked back in surprise.

"I don't believe it!" the fairy whispered. "Jack Frost is afraid of the dark!"

Sleepy
Jack Frost!

"There's no such thing as a Night Monster," Rachel explained to Jack Frost. "Look, we'll show you!"

Sabrina flew across the room and pointed her wand at the closet. The doors swung open, showing Jack Frost's collection of icy outfits, but there was nothing else to see. Then Kirsty and Rachel flew over to the dresser, and together they pulled open the drawers, one by one.

"See?" Kirsty said. "There's nothing in there!"

"What about under the bed?" Jack Frost asked suspiciously.

Sabrina, Rachel, and Kirsty linked hands and flew right under the bed from one side to the other.

"Nothing!" Sabrina said. "And there aren't any monsters in your slippers, either!"

But Jack Frost didn't look convinced. "Those Night Monsters are clever," he grumbled. "They can hide anywhere, and then pop up when I'm not expecting it!"

"There is one thing I can do to keep the Night Monsters away," Sabrina told him.

"What?" Jack Frost demanded eagerly.

"If you give me my bag of magic dream dust, I can sprinkle some around your bedroom and use my fairy magic to make sure you only have good dreams, never bad," Sabrina explained. "Then all the Night Fairies will have their bags back, and nighttime everywhere will be peaceful and quiet, and there'll be

nothing to be scared of! What do you think?"

Jack Frost hesitated, clutching his pillow.

"You could have wonderful dreams," Rachel chimed in. "You could dream that you're king of Fairyland."

"And that all the fairies are waiting on you hand and foot!" Kirsty added.

Jack Frost grinned. "Yes, that sounds like fun," he said. "Much better

than lying awake listening for Night
Monsters!"

Jack Frost reached inside the pillowcase
and pulled out the satin bag of magic
dream dust. Sabrina breathed a huge
sigh of relief as she flew over and took it
from him. Untying the drawstring, she
took a handful of dust
and scattered it
around the room. As
Rachel and Kirsty
watched, purple
sparkles filled the
room, floating from
the ceiling to the floor
like a shower of snowflakes.

Looking sleepy now, Jack Frost
snuggled down under his covers. Sabrina,
Rachel, and Kirsty picked up his teddy

bear and tucked it in beside him.

"Thank you," Jack Frost murmured dreamily. A few minutes later, he was sound asleep and snoring so peacefully

that Rachel and Kirsty couldn't help each blowing him a good-night kiss. "We did it, girls!" Sabrina whispered happily as Jack Frost snored. "Now all the Night Fairies will be able to do their nighttime work. It's time to go back to the Fairyland Palace to celebrate! But first . . ."

Sabrina flew to an open window. Taking a pinch of shimmering purple

dream dust from her bag, she gently blew it onto the breeze. Rachel and Kirsty watched the dream dust shoot out into the night, swirling toward the Fairyland Palace in the distance.

"Now everyone in Fairyland will know I have my bag back," Sabrina said with a smile. "And there won't be any more bad dreams anywhere tonight! Thank you for all your help, girls. Now, let's go. I think there will be a surprise waiting for us!"

Sweet Dreams

As Sabrina, Kirsty, and Rachel arrived
back at the palace, they heard the sound
of clapping and cheering. They floated
down into the palace gardens and
saw the king and queen and the other
Night Fairies waiting for them. They
were sitting on the palace lawn on soft
comforters and blankets with pillows to
rest their heads on.

"Welcome to our party under the stars!" Queen Titania called to Sabrina and the girls as they fluttered down to join them. They landed on one of the cozy blankets and made themselves comfortable.

"Well done!" King Oberon smiled at Sabrina, Kirsty, Rachel, and the other Night Fairies. "If it weren't for all of you, Jack Frost would still be master of the night."

"Poor Jack Frost," Sabrina said with a sigh. "He only stole the bags because he's scared of the dark!"

"Really?" The queen looked amazed. "So why did he play all those other tricks, like moving the stars around and turning the sunset green?"

"I think Jack Frost decided he might as well have some fun causing chaos with our magic dust!" Sabrina replied.

"But he won't make any more mischief now, because he's fast asleep," Kirsty said with a grin. "Sabrina gave him lots of sweet dreams!"

Everyone began to talk and laugh about all the adventures they'd had, trying to get the bags of magic dust back from the goblins. Meanwhile, Ava the Sunset Fairy and Morgan the Midnight Fairy began handing out plates of star-shaped cookies and mugs of hot chocolate with whipped cream. The girls had a wonderful time! But when Rachel spotted the fairies beginning to yawn

and Anna the Moonbeam Fairy
curling up on her blanket to go to
sleep, she knew it was time for them to
head home.

"I think we'd better go," Rachel
told the king and queen. "Thank you
so much for inviting us to the party."

"You're our guests of honor," the king
replied with a smile. "We couldn't have
found all the bags without your help."

"And we have a very special thank-you gift for you," the queen added. She handed Rachel a small satin midnight-blue pillow embroidered with a golden moon. Kirsty's was the same except that hers had a pattern of silver stars.

"The pillows are filled with a pinch of magic dust from each of the Night Fairies," the queen explained as the girls stared at the pillows with delight. "Now nighttime will always be beautiful and peaceful for you both."

"Thank you," Rachel and Kirsty said as the king and queen raised their wands. Instantly, a shower of colorful sparkles swirled around the girls as they waved good-bye to their fairy friends.

A few seconds later, the girls found that they were back to their human size and standing at the edge of the Whispering Woods in the pale moonlight. Owls hooted softly as Rachel and Kirsty tiptoed through Camp Stargaze.

"It looks like everyone's sleeping soundly now," Kirsty whispered with satisfaction. She slipped into her sleeping bag and then put her head down on the pillow the queen had given her. Rachel did the same.

"Sweet dreams, Kirsty!" Rachel said with a smile.

"Sweet dreams, Rachel!" Kirsty replied,

winking at her friend.

And in a moment or two, both girls were fast asleep, dreaming of their magical adventures with their friends the Night Fairies.

SPECIAL EDITION

Don't miss Rachel and Kirsty's
other magical adventures!
Take a look at this special sneak peek of

Cara

the Camp Fairy!

Goblin Tracks

"I can't believe we're actually at summer camp together!" Rachel Walker said happily.

"Me, neither," said her best friend, Kirsty Tate. "We get to do some of our favorite things all in one place. And we get to do them together!"

Rachel and Kirsty had met on

vacation on beautiful Rainspell Island. Since they lived in different towns, they didn't get to see each other every day. So when the girls' parents had suggested they go to Camp Oakwood, both Rachel and Kirsty were excited.

Now, on their second day of camp, the two girls sat at a table in the Craft Cabin. They were making pictures with yarn.

"First, sketch your picture on the paper," explained Bollie, their camp counselor. Bollie's real name was Margaret Bolleran, but everyone called her Bollie.

Rachel sketched a fairy on her paper. She looked over at Kirsty and saw that she had sketched a fairy, too. The girls smiled at each other.

"Now spread the glue over the places you would normally color in," Bollie said. "Then you can curl up pieces of yarn and place them on the glue, like this."

She held up a picture of a tree with green yarn for leaves and brown yarn on the trunk . . . but then the yarn slid off and plopped on one of Bollie's boots.

"That's weird," she said, feeling the paper. "This glue isn't sticky at all."

"My glue isn't sticking, either," a red-haired girl complained.

Bollie frowned. "Maybe it's too hot," she said, pushing her blonde bangs out of her eyes. "I know! Let's have some fun with the paint spinner, instead."

Bollie walked to a big machine on a table on the side of the room. Rachel, Kirsty, and the other girls gathered

around to watch.

"It's easy," Bollie said, her green eyes shining. "You put paper on the bottom. Then you turn on the spinner and squeeze in drops of paint."

She held a plastic bottle of orange paint over the spinner and squeezed it. With a *pop*, the cover slipped off! Instead of a few drops, the whole bottle of paint gushed into the spinner.

"Everybody duck!" Bollie yelled.

Rachel and Kirsty ducked down as quickly as they could. Orange paint splattered everywhere! Bollie turned off the machine, but not before every camper was covered in orange dots.

"Oh, no!" some of the girls wailed. Rachel giggled. "It's like we're covered in sprinkles," she said.

But Bollie did not look happy. "Everybody head to the sinks to clean up!" she told them. "Craft time is cancelled. We're going on a hike!"

The campers quickly washed off the paint and changed into clean green-and-white Camp Oakwood tank tops. They lined up at the edge of the woods.

"Follow me, and stick to the path," Bollie advised them.

Rachel and Kirsty hung back at the end of the line.

"Rachel, why do you think that happened in the Craft Cabin?" Kirsty asked in a whisper.

Rachel gave her a meaningful look. "It feels like Jack Frost to me."

RAINBOW magic ™

There's Magic in Every Series!

The Rainbow Fairies
The Weather Fairies
The Jewel Fairies
The Pet Fairies
The Fun Day Fairies
The Petal Fairies
The Dance Fairies
The Music Fairies
The Sports Fairies
The Party Fairies
The Ocean Fairies
The Night Fairies

Read them all!

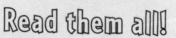

www.scholastic.com
www.rainbowmagiconline.com

HIT entertainment

RMFAI

RAINBOW magic™

SPECIAL EDITION

Three Books in Each One—
More Rainbow Magic Fun!